I dedicate this book to Rebecca,
Zachary, my many grandchildren,
and the child in us all.
Love,
Granny Lee

Every morning
Granny Lee
takes a walk
to get some
fresh air.
Before she goes,
she brews some
coffee and says
a prayer.

It feels nice to stretch her legs and see the new day begin, so before going outside, she checks on the weather to see if '

sun,

rain,

or wind.

Today it is sunny, so she wears shorts and a t-shirt,

then heads outside to first water her flowers with a squirt.

Mr. whiskers, who lives across the street,
is a sweet Orange cat.
He rubs up against her legs
then flops down for a pat.

He's everybody's friend,
but scaring the birds in their bath,
they fly away quickly,
so he lays down for a nap.

Around the next corner, in front of his house,
lives a big Rottweiler named Harlo, who carries a ball in his snout.

He's very scary to look at because he's so big,
but wouldn't hurt a person, let alone a mouse or a pig.

She then ambles to the left around the next block,
where she finds a neighbor lady working in her yard by the walk.

She stops to say hello, and as they admire the flowers, visit on and on for what seems like hours.

As she pulls herself away, she wanders up to the park, admiring the trees, flowers, and shrubbery people have in their yard.

The park is so lovely, with trees reaching the sky,
and birds, grass, and squirrels so pleasing to the eye.

A bushy tailed squirrel
scampers up the
backside of a tree,
as he hides from
a dog who would
merrily chase
him with glee.

As she proceeds down from the park as it's Granny Lee's habit,
she comes across some neighbors trying to catch their pet rabbit.
He refuses to be caught, as he hops all about,
being very happy that the kids let him out.

Watering his flowers, as I pass by his house,

I catch Mr. Ted by surprise and almost get doused.

As she rounds the next bend, and into her yard slowing her pace,

She says a prayer to God, and thanks him,
for the love of pets, people, and nature,
within her heart he has placed.

Granny Lee lives in Oregon and enjoys gardening, biking, hiking, cooking, and spending time with all of her beloved children and grandchildren.

Kelly, Lee, author
Jones, Anna, illustrator
Granny Lee goes for a walk

ISBN 9798361204021
Printed and bound in the USA

Made in the USA
Middletown, DE
24 November 2022

15686443R00015